Malik And The Magnificent Glowing Light

To Bernie,

Always remember to read a good book!

Dr. Vince Johnson

3-16-04

This Book
Belongs To:

_____

Malik And The Magnificent Glowing Light

By

Vincent L. Johnson

Malik And The Magnificent Glowing Light

Published by

PO Box 721462 Berkley, MI 48072-0462

Manufactured in United States of America.
Library of Congress Catalog Number: 97-92998
ISBN: 0-9657033-0-4

In memory of my father,
Lucian Johnson
(August 12, 1925 —April 1, 1996)
whose image graces these pages

Malik was a little boy who liked to have fun. He would run on the sidewalk, jump over puddles and wrestle and play with his friends. He also enjoyed

helping his mother around the house. But most of all, he liked doing cool
things with his dad.

Malik's father was a construction worker. He usually worked long hours, so he couldn't always spend time with Malik. Once in a while, Malik wished that he could have his father all to himself.

Sometimes he would daydream about doing special things with his dad.

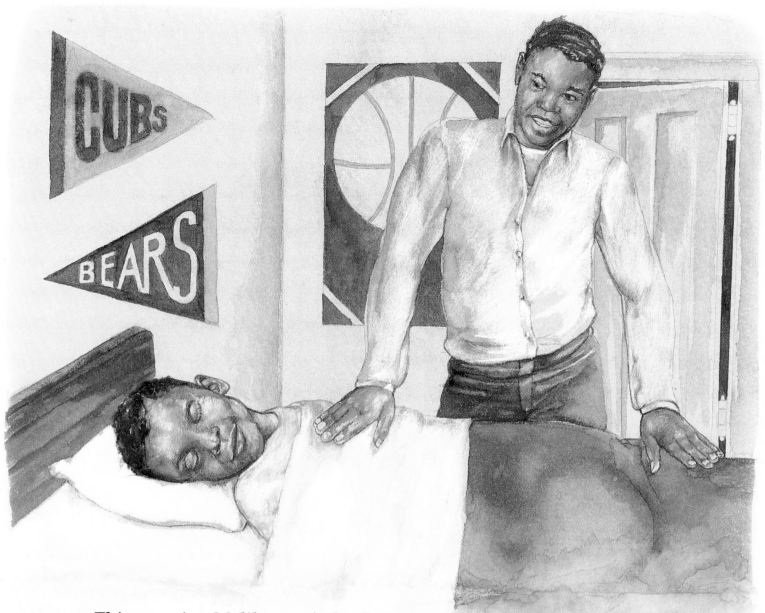

This morning Malik wasn't daydreaming because he was running late for school.

"Malik, Malik, wake up!" his father called.

Malik slowly opened his sleepy eyes and caught a peek at the sun shining into his room. "Man, it's time for school," he thought. He jumped up and ran right past his father.

"Malik, have you forgotten how to say good morning?"

"Oh, sorry, Dad, but I think I might miss the school bus. Anyway, my teacher, Miss Sanders, is going to show us a special science project."

When Malik arrived at school, Miss Sanders went to the back room, brought out a small brown box and placed it on her desk.

"Get ready class. I've got a surprise for you!"

Everyone was excited. Miss Sanders unhooked a latch on the front of the box, then she opened it. There was a long black object with red, blue, and yellow wires sticking every which way. Whatever it was, it looked weird. The only thing Malik could recognize was the two batteries on top.

"What is that?" someone shouted.

"Whatever it is, it runs on batteries," Malik said.

"It's a flashlight," Miss Sanders replied. She pointed out all the pieces. "You need a light bulb, some batteries, some wire, a piece of wood, and tape, too."

Of all the students in the classroom, Malik was the most excited. He practically jumped from his seat.

"Please make it work, Miss Sanders. Please!" he shouted. "Please!"

14

Miss Sanders turned a shiny switch. Suddenly, a golden glow began to appear in the bulb. First it was a dim red, then a dingy looking orange, and it slowly changed to a shiny bright yellow. Malik's heart began to pound quicker and quicker by the second.

The light got brighter and brighter and filled the entire room with a magnificent glow. When Miss Sanders turned off the light, Malik shouted, "Can we build a flashlight?"

"Well the flashlight is our project for next week. Today, we're going to study the different shapes of leaves," Miss Sanders said. Why would his teacher show such a cool project, then give them something else to do? Why couldn't they make the flashlight today?

Miss Sanders began to pass out the leaves, but Malik had something else on his mind. He just stared at the leaf in front of him. Malik was so bored that he couldn't wait to get home.

When the school bus reached Malik's house, he jumped off and ran
as fast as he could straight to his bedroom. He just had to think of how the flashlight
was made. "Let's see. There was a light bulb and some batteries, but what else?"

First, he began searching for a light bulb. Malik ran over the house looking
around the kitchen and in the bathroom. Finally he thought,
"I'll check out the pantry." The pantry was filled with boxes of old clothes.
"I bet there's some stuff in those boxes that I could use to build a flashlight,"
he thought.

He jumped on top of the clothes and began to crawl around. Suddenly the boxes felt strange. He sank to the floor making a loud crash. Whoomp! Boomp! Kaboomp! Clothes flew into the air. Hats and shirts, blouses and sweaters, shoes and socks covered Malik.

When he worked his way back to the top, he was wearing the strangest looking hat and one of his mother's old blouses.

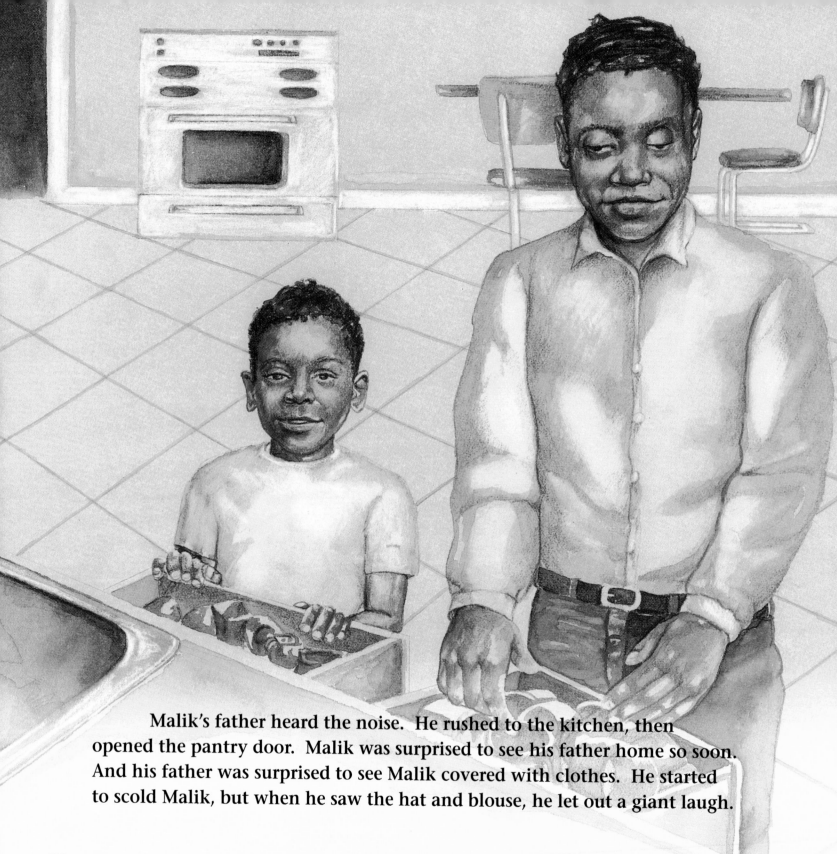

Malik's father heard the noise. He rushed to the kitchen, then opened the pantry door. Malik was surprised to see his father home so soon. And his father was surprised to see Malik covered with clothes. He started to scold Malik, but when he saw the hat and blouse, he let out a giant laugh.

"Ha, ha, ha, Malik, how did you get yourself into this mess?"

"I was trying to get to those boxes in the back, Dad."

"What's in those boxes that you could want, Malik?"

"Well, today at school, Miss Sanders showed us this really cool flashlight, then she told us that we would have a different project."

"What kind of project?" his father asked.

"Leaves, Dad. Can you believe that? We're going to make a flashlight next week, but I just can't get my mind off that flashlight. When Miss Sanders turned it on, the light filled the whole room!"

"Well, we could probably make a flashlight, Malik. But you need to do your homework first."

Malik must have set a record for completing his work. After his father checked the homework, they started searching for items to use for a flashlight. Malik was delighted that he would get to spend more time with his dad.

"Okay, Malik, what do we need to build our flashlight?"

"Some wire, some batteries, — let's see — a light bulb, some tape, a piece of wood. And, oh yeah, we need a switch too, Dad."

Malik and his father searched the drawers in the kitchen and the nooks and crannies in the bathroom. They even looked through the boxes in the pantry.

When they were finished, they found a small light bulb, a piece of wood, some batteries, one short piece of wire and an old rusty switch. But they couldn't find any tape.

"Dad, Miss Sanders had tape."

"Well, maybe we can use a piece of string instead, Malik."

His father went to the kitchen and found an old shoestring. Then they began connecting the wire to the light bulb. They used the shoestring to tie the batteries to the wood.

When they were finished, their flashlight didn't look like the one at school. It looked like a light from outer space. But Malik didn't seem to mind. He wanted to build a flashlight, and that's exactly what they did.

Malik was afraid to touch the flashlight. What if it didn't work? What if he broke it? But now was the time to see if the flashlight worked. Malik began to tremble as he brought his hand closer and closer to the switch. Finally, he turned it on, but it didn't work.

"Dad, what's the matter? Why won't the flashlight work?"

"I don't know. Everything seems to be connected. Maybe the batteries don't work. And if it's the batteries, we can buy new ones tomorrow. Besides, its getting close to your bedtime."

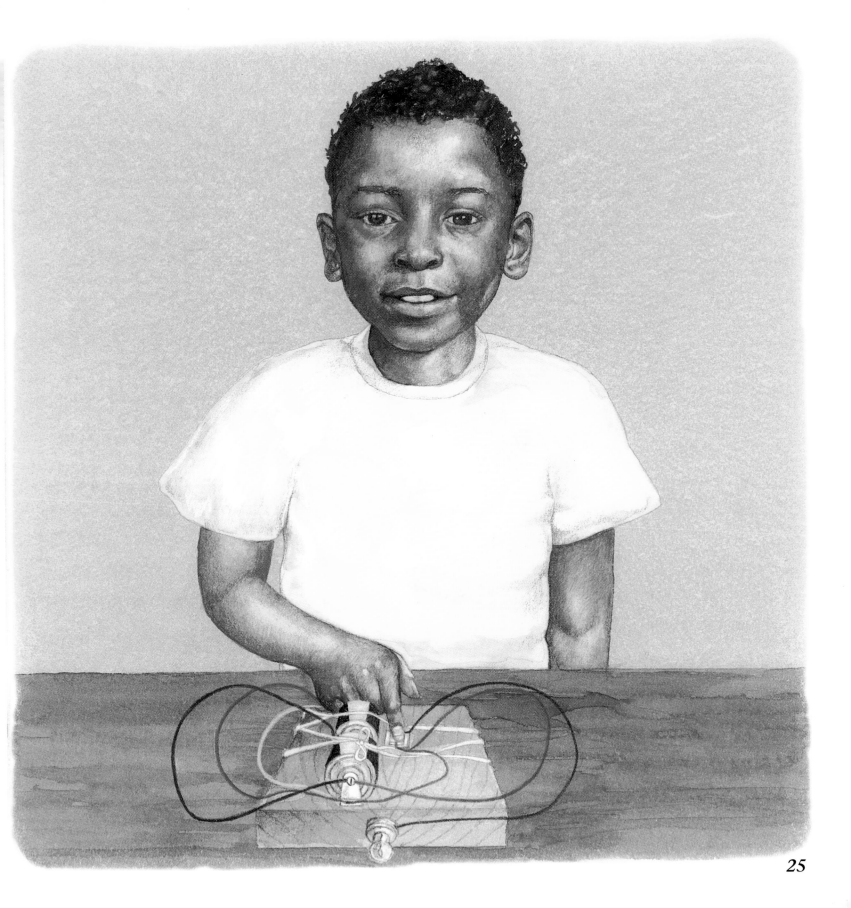

Malik didn't know what to do. He wanted the flashlight to work now, not tomorrow. Suddenly, he remembered one of his battery-operated trucks. "Now these batteries have to work," he thought.

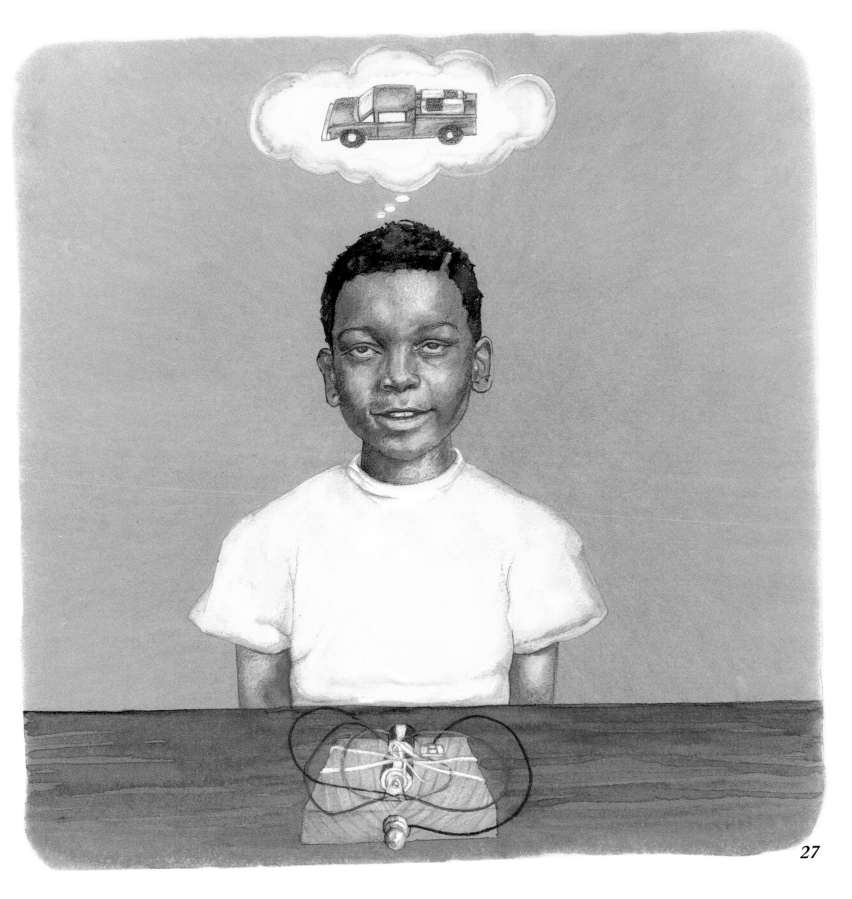

When the batteries were changed, Malik slowly reached for the switch and turned it. He couldn't believe his eyes. First there was a dim red, then a dingy looking orange, and it slowly changed to a shiny bright yellow. The flashlight worked!

The light got brighter and brighter until the entire room was filled with a magnificent glow. Malik was so happy that he grinned from ear to ear. "We did it! WE DID IT!" he shouted.

When Malik went to bed all he dreamed about was lights: sunlight, starlight, moonlight, but the one light that really stayed in his mind was the glowing flashlight.

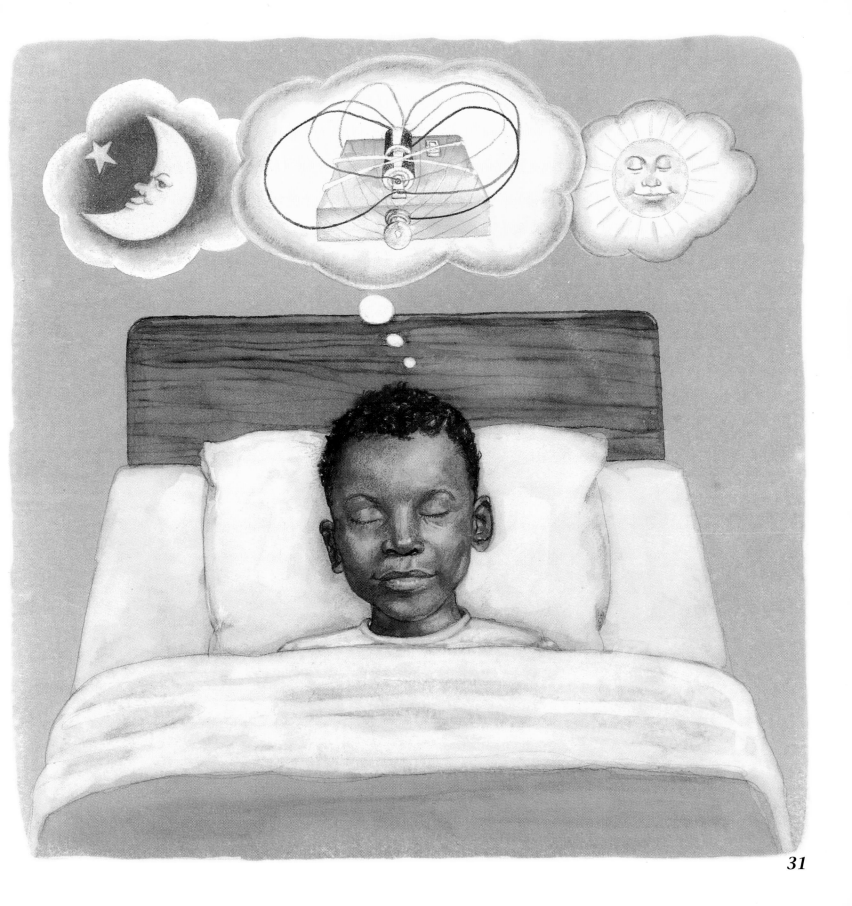

When Malik got to school the next day, he couldn't wait to show the flashlight to his class.

"Hey everybody, I've got a surprise for you," Malik shouted.

"Malik, do you have something to share with the class?" Miss Sanders said.

Malik took the flashlight from his bag and laid it on his desk.

"What's that?" someone shouted.

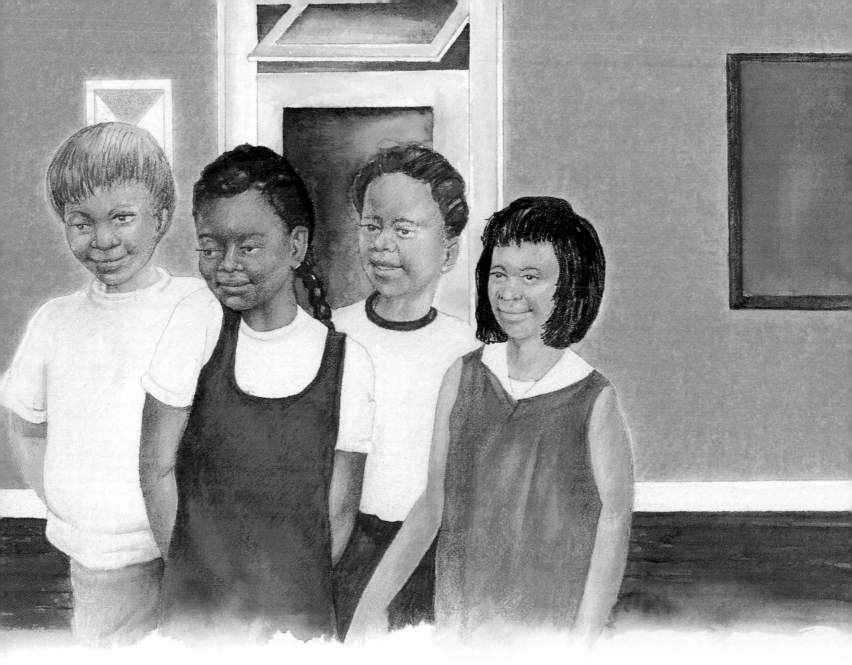

"I'll show you." Malik replied. He turned the switch, and suddenly a light appeared. Everyone in the class nearly jumped from their seats. First it was a dim red, then a dingy looking orange, and it slowly changed to a shiny bright yellow.

The light got brighter and brighter until the entire room was filled with a magnificent glow. Malik stared at the light with a smile. He was proud that he and his father had built such a magnificent glowing light.

Photo by Efua Korantema

Vincent L. Johnson grew up on the west side of Chicago where he was inspired to write short stories, essays, and poetry from the age of twelve. *Malik and the Magnificent Glowing Light* is a reflection of one of his childhood experiences and draws upon the relationship he shared with his father. Vincent pursued his college education at Loyola University Chicago where he received a Bachelor of Science degree in biology. Later he attended Loyola University Stritch School of Medicine, where he earned his Doctor of Medicine degree. He currently practices Internal Medicine and Pediatrics.